GRAPHIC SHAKESPEAR
A Midsummer Night's Dream

CONTENTS

Published by
Evans Brothers Limited
2A Portman Mansions
Chiltern Street
London W1M 1LE

© in the modern text Hilary Burningham 1999
© in the illustrations Evans Brothers Ltd 1999
Designed by Design Systems Ltd.

British Library Cataloguing in Publication Data
Burningham, Hilary
  A midsummer night's dream
  Teacher's book. – (The graphic Shakespeare series)
  1. Shakespeare, William, 1564-1616. Midsummer night's dream
  2. Shakespeare, William, 1564-1616 – Study and teaching
  (Secondary)
  I. Title II. Slattery, Zara
  822.3'3

  ISBN 0 237 51968 2

Printed in Hong Kong by Wing King Tong Co. Ltd.

*The author and publisher would like to thank Susan Tranter and
the management of Shakespeare's Globe for kindly allowing Neil Deans
to sketch the interior of the theatre.*

INTRODUCTION TO THE GRAPHIC
A MIDSUMMER NIGHT'S DREAM ACTIVITY BOOK

William Shakespeare's *A Midsummer Night's Dream* is one of the world's favourite plays. An inspired mix of love interest, buffoonery, magic and mystery, coupled with a masterful use of the English language shape a comic drama that engages the audience at every level. The tradesmen provide slapstick comedy, the young people fall in and out of love with great intensity, while the world of the fairies has a magical, dreamlike quality. The characters operate as foils for each other, and as the action moves from tradesmen, to lovers, to fairyland, the tempo and rhythm of the play quickens and slows with spellbinding variety. Shakespeare's language is in turn delicate, soaring, forceful or boisterous. To all this is added the impish, mercurial Puck who comments with glee on the foibles of the helpless mortals.

Dream is about all kinds of love. Duke Theseus and Hippolyta are savouring the delights and anticipation of mature love. They now meet on an equal footing having been respected adversaries in battle. They are old enough to know what they're doing, yet young enough to enjoy the undoubted physical attraction between them. Titania and Oberon similarly have a strong, mutual physical attraction. At their first meeting, the memorable phrases, "Ill met by moonlight...." and, "Tarry, rash wanton......" crackle with the frustrated emotion. Oberon wants something and cannot understand why Titania refuses to let him have his way. She is deliberately humiliated when made to fall in love with an ass – yet in the end doesn't seem to mind. Oberon has his way, and becomes "My Oberon" again to the besotted Titania.

In the manipulation of the lovers, via the juice of the magic flower, Shakespeare explores one of his favourite themes: the way the chemistry of love alters both vision and perception. The physical application of magic juice to the eyes of the lovers underlines that what we call "falling in love" in fact involves a bio-chemical reaction. Unlike, say, *Romeo and Juliet*, the lovers in *Dream* are caught up in a relatively light-hearted situation. There are no suggestions of tragic outcomes. These are privileged, spirited young people who, if the current romances didn't work out would probably have little difficulty finding other, suitable mates. Hermia's nasty alternatives, obey her father or be sent to a nunnery or, worse, be put to death do not appear to dwell unduly on her mind. Even the major row between Hermia and Helena provokes laughter as Hermia dwells on Helena's height: "thou painted maypole", and, "she hath urged her height". Hermia hangs on to Lysander for dear life: "get off, thou cat, thou burr," he shouts in frustration. In many staged or filmed productions the lovers end up rolling on the ground, covered in mud – hardly high tragedy.

Puck's chattered commentary also serves to underline that these lovers' quarrels and misunderstandings are not to be taken too seriously. Lines such as: "And those things do best please me That befall preposterously," or, "....yet but three? Come one more – Two of both kinds make up four," have a 'rimey-dimey' quality with echoes of the nursery.

These activities, therefore, have been devised to reinforce the simple text in the pupil's book and to help students to keep the various plots, sub-plots and groups of characters sorted out. It is vitally important, nevertheless, to use every opportunity to encourage students to read Shakespeare's language aloud. Understanding every word is less important than opening the mind and the voice to the powerful images and strong rhythms.

The National Literacy Strategy
The National Literacy Strategy has helped to shape this teacher's book. Many Year 6 teachers will wish to take up the challenge of "the possibility of pupils studying a Shakespeare play in Year 6, where appropriate". With the help of these adapted texts and the related activities, all pupils will be able to gain an understanding of what is happening in the play and can begin to access Shakespeare's language by reading short, manageable chunks in the form of the Key Speeches on each page. Shakespeare's language, sometimes with accompanying paraphrase in modern English, is also used extensively throughout the worksheets. Students will be encouraged to read aloud some of the most beautiful, poetic, or amusing speeches.

In keeping with the National Literacy Strategy, there is some formal analysis of Shakespeare's language, especially alliteration, of which there is a great deal in *A Midsummer Night's Dream*, and examples of the rich diversity of adjectives and adverbs. As secondary schools will be expected to reinforce and progress the National Literacy Strategy, secondary pupils can also benefit from the activities.

The Student Activities

The aim of the activities in this book is to reinforce learning by emphasising elements of plot and characterisation, ensuring that pupils have a good understanding of what is actually happening in the play. The majority of the activities are sufficiently straightforward to enable any student to work independently, or with peer/adult support, and produce a respectable piece of work. Whenever possible, they should be encouraged to read work aloud in order to reinforce good writing habits and sentence structure.

There are opportunities for expanding the work on the play by producing a scene for performance: *The Comedy of Pyramus and Thisbe* is suggested. A variety of related activities - organising and running rehearsals, producing publicity materials, devising appropriate costumes and props and expressing appreciation - provide important learning opportunities. Specific suggestions are included on pages 33 and 34.

Activities that promote discussion and also include an element of peer group teaching are: *Desktop Teaching* (pages 40 and 41) and the *"Who Am I?"* game (pages 42 to 46). These are both excellent revision techniques, once the students have an overview of the play. The pictures from the Portrait Gallery can also be matched with a selection of Key Speeches, under the heading of *"Who Said That?"*

Attainment Levels

In keeping with the aims of the National Curriculum, and to promote effective monitoring and record-keeping, appropriate attainment levels are suggested for each activity. It should be noted that in general the attainment levels given for Reading (Attainment Target 2:AT2) are higher than those for Writing (AT3). This is because Shakespeare's text, even with the aids and prompts that are given, demands a good level of reading comprehension. Keeping in mind that AT2 emphasises responses to a range of texts, the work on Shakespeare needs to be seen as part of the balanced selection of literature that the pupil will study in the course of the year. Understanding Shakespeare's language will contribute to the pupil's attaining up to Level 5. Higher levels at AT3 can be achieved by opting for the more challenging tasks.

The Student Record Sheet

It is not suggested that every student should complete every activity in the book. Rather it is the intention to provide manageable tasks at each stage of the play so that the teacher has available suitable materials for the student who needs or can benefit from them. An added bonus is that a student notebook or file containing a selection of completed activities provides a good framework for revision or basis for projects or course work. The Student Record Sheet gives all-important opportunities for self-assessment. The student enters the number and title of each worksheet and evaluates how well it was completed. There is also a column for the degree of ease or difficulty, as assessed by the student. If too many are classified as "easy", it is clearly time to move to more challenging work. There is a final column for teacher comment.

Celebrating Shakespeare

At the conclusion of the work on *A Midsummer Night's Dream*, students can celebrate their work by putting on a "living exhibition". Wall or display board mounted work could include: posters for the play, maps of Athens and the woods, written work, including the Points of View Activity (page 39), accompanied by portraits of the characters. As part of a "living exhibition", students also memorise their favourite speeches, take the parts of their favourite characters, and show guests around the exhibition. Some pupils might like to do research into Greek food. What sort of "packed lunch" might Theseus and Hippolyta have taken with them on a day's hunting?

There can be no substitute for the excitement of a Shakespeare play performed live on stage. *The Graphic Shakespeare Series* aims to make his work more accessible to readers having various cultural backgrounds and levels of ability in the hope that they will be encouraged to explore further, developing their appreciation and new skills in the process. The books in the series are not meant as an end in themselves, but as a beginning.

SHAKESPEARE'S GLOBE
One Man's Dream

In Shakespeare's time, several theatres or playhouses were located on the south bank of the Thames, roughly opposite St. Paul's Cathedral. We know the names of the playhouses: The Rose, The Swan, The Hope and The Globe. Unfortunately, none of them has survived to the present day. We have to try to learn about them from old drawings and from some of the remains and outlines that have been found in the ground.

Since 1997, visitors to London have been able to see plays in a theatre built in the same style, with the same materials, as the theatres that Shakespeare knew. They were built almost entirely of wood. Shakespeare's Globe is situated beside the Thames, very close to where the original Globe once stood.

It took almost thirty years, first obtaining the land, then raising the money, to rebuild Shakespeare's Globe in London. It was one man's lifetime dream. He was an American named Sam Wanamaker. Sam Wanamaker was the man who made it all happen. Sadly, he died before the theatre was officially opened, but his dream has become a reality.

Shakespeare's Globe is sometimes called 'The Wooden O' because it is built of wood and is round with the centre open to the sky. Plays are put on during the summer months, but the theatre can be visited at any time of the year. When one enters The Globe, the huge stage rises majestically, painted in beautiful, vivid colours. It glows with reds, earth colours, rich turquoise, marbled effects, and gold leaf. Circling the theatre are the balconies, three rows of them, where the audience sits. People can also stand on the ground around the stage, just as they did in Shakespeare's time. Why do you think these people are called *groundlings*? What happens to groundlings when it rains?

Shakespeare's groundlings were very noisy – eating and drinking all through the play, and calling out and making noises. Today's groundlings are sometimes noisy too. The actors have to work very hard indeed. The audience surrounds them on three sides, and they have to move around so that everyone can see and hear them. Most of all, they have to keep the attention of those noisy groundlings.

EGEUS WAS ANGRY WITH HIS DAUGHTER

In this scene, you meet some of the characters in *A Midsummer Night's Dream*.
With a partner, or working in a small group, fill each space in the sentences below with the name
of the correct character in the play. You may have to use some names more than once.

1. _____ was to marry the Queen of the Amazons.

2. _____, Queen of the Amazons, was to marry Theseus, the

   _____ of Athens.

3. _____ was the father of Hermia.

4. _____ was angry with his daughter.

5. _____ wanted everyone to be happy and enjoy his wedding.

6. _____ was in love with Lysander.

7. _____ did not want to marry Demetrius.

8. _____ told Hermia to do as her father wished.

9. _____ told the Duke about his problems with his daughter.

10. _____ was told that she would be put to death or sent to live in a nunnery. That was
    the law of Athens.

Egeus   Lysander   Theseus   Demetrius   Hermia   Duke

Point to talk about: Read aloud number 10. What is your opinion of this law of Athens? Can you think of some
good points and some bad points?

AT 1:4
AT 3:2

LYSANDER'S PLAN

Lysander had a plan. He and Hermia could run away together to the home of his rich aunt.
Look at the table below. Lysander's plan is written for you in Modern English.
Write the words in Shakespeare's English that match each part of the plan.
Read the plan aloud, first in Modern English, then in Shakespeare's English.

Modern English	Shakespeare's English
I have a rich aunt whose husband has died, and she has no children.	
Her house is seven leagues away from Athens, and she loves me as if I were her only son.	
There, at my aunt's home, dear Hermia, I would like to marry you, where we will be away from the strict laws of Athens.	
If you love me, then, quietly leave your father's house tomorrow night, and in the wood a short distance outside the town I will wait for you.	

Shakespeare's English
From Athens is her house remote seven leagues[1]; And she respects me as her only son.
I have a widow aunt, a dowager, Of great revenue; and she hath no child.
If thou lovest me, then Steal forth thy father's house tomorrow night, And in the wood, a league without the town – There will I stay for thee.
There, gentle Hermia, may I marry thee; And to that place the sharp Athenian law cannot pursue us.

---

[1] league - an old measure of distance, about 5 kilometres.

HELENA'S PLAN

> Helena met Hermia and Lysander. She asked Hermia to "teach" her how to get Demetrius's love.
> Choose two members of your class or group to read the following lines together.
> Notice how Helena picked up Hermia's words, showing that she was trying to be like her.
> Hermia ended by saying that she and Lysander were going to run away. This gave Helena an idea.....

HELENA: **O, teach me how you look, and with what art**
You sway the motion of Demetrius' heart.

HERMIA: **I frown upon him, yet he loves me still.**

HELENA: **O that your frowns would teach my smiles such skill!**

HERMIA: **I give him curses, yet he gives me love.**

HELENA: **O that my prayers could such affection move!**

HERMIA: **The more I hate, the more he follows me.**

HELENA: **The more I love, the more he hateth me.**

HERMIA: **His folly, Helena, is no fault of mine.**

HELENA: **None but your beauty. Would that fault were mine!**

HERMIA: **Take comfort. He no more shall see my face,**
Lysander and myself will fly this place.

The lines contain some *opposites*.
Can you find the opposite of:

frowns   _____

prayers   _____

love   _____

The Plan

> Helena decided to tell Demetrius that Hermia and Lysander were going to run away.
> She hoped he would be grateful, and love her again.

HELENA: **I will go tell him of fair Hermia's flight.**
Then to the wood will he tomorrow night
Pursue her; and for this intelligence
If I have thanks it is a dear expense.
But herein mean I to enrich my pain,
To have his sight thither, and back again.

Words to help you:
pursue *means* follow
intelligence *means* information
sight *in this case, means* love

Keep a Word List

Note: as you read the play and do the worksheets, keep a list of new words and their meanings on a separate sheet of paper. From time to time, ask a friend, teacher or parent to test you on the words – checking for both spelling and meaning.

AT 2:5

PUTTING ON A PLAY

> Working with a partner or in a small group, read pages 14, 16 and 18 in
> *The Graphic Midsummer Night's Dream.*
> Decide on the answers to the following questions and write them in your notebook.

1. Who were the people practising a play?

2. When did they hope to put on their play?

3. What was the title of the play?

4. Who was the leader of the group?

5. Who thought he could play all the parts better than anyone else?

6. Why didn't Flute want to take the part of Thisbe?

7. Who was to take the part of the lion?

8. When was the next rehearsal to take place?

9. Where was the next rehearsal to take place?

10. What were the tradesmen supposed to do before the next rehearsal?

Act 1, Scene 2 is a wonderful scene to act out.

Clear a space in your classroom to use as a stage.

Choose members of the class to play the parts of the tradesmen – Quince, Snug, Bottom, Flute, Snout, and Starveling.

Quince is the leader of the group. Today, we would call him the Director of the play. He gets very exasperated with Bottom, who is constantly interrupting.

Bottom is a show-off. He swaggers around the stage, telling everyone else what to do, and acting out all the parts. He is quite sure he can play all the parts better than anyone else.

Flute plays the part of Thisbe. He is worried about having a beard coming. When Quince tells him "you may speak as small as you will", he means that Flute should speak in a high voice. Bottom, of course, wants to be Thisbe. When he says he will speak "in a monstrous little voice", he makes his voice very high and squeaky.

Snug is "slow of study", and would speak quite slowly. The lion's part suits him very well, since all he has to do is roar.

Starveling and **Snout** have only one line each in this scene, but they must appear interested and listen carefully to Quince and the others. They look as though they're getting fed up with Bottom's interruptions.

AT 3:3

INTRODUCING PUCK

Read aloud page 20 in *The Graphic Midsummer Night's Dream*, then look at the sentences below. Some of them are True, and some of them are False. Write each sentence in your notebook, followed by the words True or False. Read the sentences and your answers aloud.
If you have time, try making the True sentences False, and the False sentences True!

1. Puck served Oberon, the King of the Fairies.

2. The King and Queen of the Fairies were good friends.

3. Oberon had taken a young boy to be his attendant.

4. The King and Queen of the Fairies were being very rude to each other.

5. Puck's other name was Robin Goodfellow.

6. Puck was a very serious sort of fellow.

7. Puck always brought bad luck to people.

8. The fairy was happy and excited because Oberon and Titania were coming.

9. Puck made Oberon laugh.

10. The Queen of the Fairies was called Titania.

Making the False, *True* and the True, *False*. Examples:

1. Puck served Oberon, the King of the Fairies. True
    Puck served Titania, the Queen of the Fairies. False

2. The King and Queen of the Fairies were good friends. False
    The King and Queen of the Fairies were having a terrible row. True

AT 3:3

— 10 —

OBERON AND TITANIA

Read page 22 in *The Graphic Midsummer Night's Dream*. Below are some of the things that Oberon and Titania said to each other in their quarrel. Can you match the meanings with their words? Draw the chart in your notebook. Put Oberon and Titania's words on one side (copy them, or cut out and paste in your book), with the correct meaning opposite.

Oberon and Titania's Words	Meaning
TITANIA: Why art thou here Come from the farthest step of India But that, forsooth, the bouncing Amazon, Your buskined mistress and your warrior love, To Theseus must be wedded? – and you come To give their bed joy and prosperity.	TITANIA: The ox and the ploughman have worked for nothing, and the corn has rotted in the field before it was ripe.
OBERON: How canst thou thus, for shame, Titania, Glance at my credit with Hippolyta, Knowing I know thy love to Theseus?	OBERON: Why won't you do as I ask? All I'm asking for is the little human[1] boy to be my servant.
TITANIA: The ox hath therefore stretched his yoke in vain, The ploughman lost his sweat, and the green corn Hath rotted ere his youth attained a beard.	TITANIA: What brings you all this way from India, except that that big Amazon woman that you love is to marry Theseus? You have come to wish them well.
TITANIA: The spring, the summer, The chiding autumn, angry winter change Their wonted liveries, and the mazed world By their increase now knows not which is which.	TITANIA: Come away, fairies, We shall have a real row if I stay here any longer.
OBERON: Why should Titania cross her Oberon? I do but beg a little changeling boy To be my henchman.	TITANIA: Don't worry. I wouldn't sell the child for all the money in fairyland.
TITANIA: Set your heart at rest. The fairy land buys not the child of me.	TITANIA: The seasons are all muddled, and people don't know where they are.
TITANIA: Fairies, away, We shall chide downright if I longer stay.	OBERON: You ought to be ashamed to talk about Hippolyta and me, knowing that I know you love Theseus.
OBERON: Ill met by moonlight, proud Titania.	OBERON: This is a bad meeting tonight, haughty Titania.

[1] A changeling, to humans, is an elf or fairy that has replaced a human child. To the fairies, a changeling would, presumably, be human.

AT 2:5

OBERON'S PLAN

The Magic Flower

Read page 24 in *The Graphic Midsummer Night's Dream*.
Read the following questions carefully and write the answers in good sentences.
When you have finished, read your answers aloud.
Draw the magic flower in your notebook, and colour it in.

---

1. What colour was the magic flower?

2. What part of the flower was magic?

3. How did the magic work?

4. Who did Oberon send to fetch the flower?

5. How did Oberon plan to use the magic flower?

Oberon's Instructions to Puck

OBERON: **Fetch me that flower – the herb I showed thee once.**
The juice of it on sleeping eyelids laid
Will make or man or woman madly dote
Upon the next live creature that it sees.

6. What do you think "madly dote upon" might mean?

OBERON WAITED FOR PUCK

Read page 26 in *The Graphic Midsummer Night's Dream*.
Read the questions below and answer them in good sentences.
Read your answers aloud. Talk about your answers to question 10.

1. Who was Oberon waiting for?

2. What was Puck bringing?

3. Why had Demetrius come to the wood?

4. Who did Demetrius meet?

5. What did Helena tell Demetrius?

6. Did Demetrius love Helena?

7. Who did Demetrius love?

8. Who else heard Demetrius and Helena's conversation?

9. In what way did Oberon think he might be able to help Helena?

10. In your opinion, why did Oberon feel sorry for Helena?

AT 3:3-4

WHO PLANNED TO BE IN THE FOREST THAT NIGHT?

Oberon planned to use the juice of the magic flower to make Demetrius fall in love with Helena.
He thought that Demetrius and Helena were the only Athenians in the woods that night. He was wrong!

HERMIA	LYSANDER	HELENA	DEMETRIUS
YES NO	YES NO	YES NO	YES NO

Cut out the pictures above and paste them in your notebook.
Decide who was planning to be in the forest that night, and circle Yes or No.
Look at the reasons given below, and write the correct reason under each picture.

"I was following Demetrius. I was hoping he would love me again."

"I was running away with Hermia. We wanted to be married."

"I was running away with Lysander. We wanted to be married."

"I was looking for Hermia. I didn't want her to marry Lysander."

Reading with Expression

Read aloud Oberon's speech below. Try to follow the directions given for you.

OBERON: **I know a bank where the wild thyme blows,**
Where oxlips and the nodding violet grows,
Quite overcanopied with luscious woodbine,
With sweet muskroses and with eglantine.
There sleeps Titania some time of the night,
Lulled in these flowers with dances and delight.
And there the snake throws her enamelled skin,
Weed wide enough to wrap a fairy in.
And with the juice of this I'll streak her eyes
And make her full of hateful fantasies.

*These lines should be
read warmly, almost
lovingly. Listen to
the beautiful sounds
of the words.*

*Oberon's voice becomes
harsh*

AT 2:5

THE FAIRIES' SONG

The fairies sang Titania to sleep with a beautiful song. The song had two verses that described the bad things that were to keep away from Titania, and a Chorus that was sung after each verse.
The Chorus was about Philomel, which is another name for the nightingale, a bird which sings very sweetly at night. Copy the verses of the song into your notebook. You need only write the Chorus once.
Decorate the page with some of the creatures in the song.

First Fairy:

You spotted snakes with double tongue,
　Thorny hedgehogs, be not seen.
Newts and blindworms, do no wrong,
　Come not near our Fairy Queen.

Second Fairy:

Weaving spiders, come not here;
　Hence, you longlegged spinners, hence!
Beetles black, approach not near,
　Worm nor snail, do no offence.

Chorus:

Philomel with melody
Sing in our sweet lullaby[1],
Lulla, lulla, lullaby; lulla, lulla, lullaby.
Never harm
Nor spell nor charm
Come our lovely lady nigh.
So good night, with lullaby.

Alliteration

Underline all the "l" sounds in the Chorus. Note: double "ll" counts as one.
How many times is "l" repeated? More than twenty times!

Repeating a sound to get a special effect is called "alliteration". The effect of the "l" sound is usually very soothing; for example, it is repeated in the word "lullaby".
Other sounds may be repeated for different reasons. Shakespeare often uses alliteration. You will be able to find more examples in the play.

Oberon Put the Magic Juice on Titania's Eyelids

Read Oberon's speech, below. He was not wishing pleasant things for Titania!
Try to memorise the speech, and say it with expression.

OBERON: **What thou seest when thou dost wake,**
　　　　Do it for thy true love take;
　　　　Love and languish for his sake.
　　　　Be it ounce or cat or bear,
　　　　Pard, or boar with bristled hair
　　　　In thy eye that shall appear
　　　　When thou wakest, it is thy dear.
　　　　Wake when some vile thing is near!

[1.] lullaby - a song to put a child or baby to sleep

PUCK'S MISTAKE

Read page 32 in *The Graphic Midsummer Night's Dream*.
Write the sentences below, choosing the correct word from the brackets to complete the meaning.
When you have finished, read your sentences aloud.

---

1. Hermia and Lysander had been wandering in the (meadow   town   forest).

2. They were very (happy   sad   tired).

3. They decided to (run   sleep   walk) until daylight.

4. Puck was looking for the young man (Oberon   Egeus   Theseus) had told him to find.

5. Puck saw (Lysander   Demetrius   Oberon) wearing Athenian clothes.

6. Puck squeezed the magic juice on (Demetrius's   Lysander's   Quince's) eyelids.

7. Puck was sure he had used the magic juice on the (right   wrong) person.

8. In fact, Puck had used the magic juice on the (right   wrong) person.

Can you make up other sentences with words to choose?
For example: Lysander loved (Hippolyta   Helena   Hermia). Ask your friends to try your sentences.

AT 3:3-4

HELENA GOT A SURPRISE

> The sentences below are not in the right order. Can you arrange them correctly?
> Page 34 in *The Graphic Midsummer Night's Dream* will help you.
> When you have finished, read your sentences aloud.

Helena was afraid Lysander might be dead.

Helena ran away and Lysander followed her.

Lysander awoke.

Helena was chasing Demetrius through the forest.

Lysander told Helena he loved her.

Demetrius ran away, leaving Helena alone.

Lysander fell madly in love with Helena.

Helena called to Lysander, to see if he was awake.

Helena thought Lysander was joking.

Helena saw Lysander on the ground.

Helena was the first person Lysander saw.

Helena's Point of View

Describe what happened in this scene from Helena's point of view.

If Helena was talking to a friend, she might begin by saying, "I was running through the forest that night, trying to catch up with Demetrius. Demetrius was being horrible! I started to feel very tired and stopped to rest. Guess who I saw lying on the ground – Lysander!..."

Continue the story, ending with, "Lysander was definitely making fun of me. I got out of there as quickly as I could."

Tell your story aloud, as if you were Helena speaking to a friend. It isn't necessary to write down every word you plan to say, so long as you have made a note of the main points you want to include.

AT 2:3
AT 1:4

HERMIA WAS ALONE

HERMIA

Draw a circle around the words below that describe how Hermia felt when she awoke alone and realised Lysander was gone. Look up the meanings of any difficult words, and add them to your word list.

lost   **lonely**   **isolated**   **happy**

frightened   **overjoyed**   **terrified**

worried   **anxious**   **lucky**

Can you think of some other words to describe how Hermia felt? Add them to your list.

Write some sentences from Hermia's point of view, describing how she was feeling.
eg
When I awoke, Lysander was nowhere to be seen. It was still dark. I was all alone. I started to call out his name, then I ...

AT 3:4

REHEARSING "PYRAMUS AND THISBE"

First, be sure you have read page 38 in *The Graphic Midsummer Night's Dream.*
Next, look at some of the things that the tradesmen were worried about when they put on their play.
Together, they worked out solutions to their problems. As usual, Bottom had the most to say.
Match the problem with the correct solution.

Problem	Solution
Pyramus must kill himself with a sword. The ladies wouldn't like it.	
Snout was worried that the ladies might be afraid of the lion.	
Pyramus and Thisbe had to meet by moonlight. How would they show moonlight in the Great Chamber[1] of the Duke's palace?	
Pyramus and Thisbe spoke to each other through a hole in a wall. How could they bring a wall into the Great Chamber?	

Solution	Solution
BOTTOM: .... you must name his name, and half his face must be seen through the lion's neck....and there indeed let him name his name, and tell them plainly he is Snug the joiner.	BOTTOM: .... let the prologue[2] seem to say we will do no harm with our swords, and that Pyramus is not killed indeed; and ...tell them that I, Pyramus, am not Pyramus, but Bottom the weaver.
BOTTOM: Some man or other must present Wall; and let him have some plaster, or some loam, or roughcast about him to signify Wall; and let him hold his fingers thus, and through that cranny shall Pyramus and Thisbe whisper.	QUINCE: .... one must come in with a bush of thorns and a lantern, and say he comes to disfigure or present the person of Moonshine.

[1] Great Chamber - a large hall in the Duke's palace for banquets and entertaining
[2] prologue - a speech at the beginning of a play, telling the audience about the play

BOTTOM GOT AN ASS'S[1] HEAD

Read pages 40 and 42 in *The Graphic Midsummer Night's Dream*.
In good sentences, answer the following questions. When you have finished, read your answers aloud.

1. Where was Bottom when Puck gave him the ass's head?

2. Did Bottom know that he was wearing an ass's head?

3. How did the other tradesmen feel?

4. What did they do?

5. What did Puck plan to do next?

6. What did Bottom do to cheer himself up?

7. What caused Titania to wake up?

8. What had Oberon put on her eyes?

9. What was the first thing that she saw when she awoke?

10. Why did she fall madly in love with Bottom?

More Alliteration

Puck described how he was going to lead Quince, Snug, Flute, and Starveling all around the forest.
Read his words, below. What sounds or letters are repeated? Underline them.
What is the effect of repeating the letter "b" for example? Or the letter "h"?
These lines are full of Puck's energy and mischief. Memorise them, and say them with lots of expression.
Clear a space in your classroom to be a stage and move around the stage as you say the words.

PUCK: **I'll follow you, I'll lead you about a round,**
Thorough bog, thorough bush, thorough brake, thorough briar,
Sometime a horse I'll be, sometime a hound,
A hog, a headless bear, sometime a fire,
And neigh, and bark, and grunt and roar and burn
Like horse, hound, hog, bear, fire at every turn.

PUCK

[1] ass - ass is another word for *donkey*

BOTTOM AND THE FAIRIES

The Four Fairies　　　　　　　　　　　　　　　　　　　AT 2:5

MOTH

PEASEBLOSSOM　　　　MUSTARDSEED　　　　COBWEB

Cut out the pictures of the fairies.
Write or cut out and paste Bottom's words beside the appropriate fairy.
Read aloud Bottom's speeches.

BOTTOM: **I shall desire you of more acquaintance, good Master Cobweb – if I cut my finger I shall make bold with you!**

BOTTOM: **I pray you commend me to Mistress Squash, your mother, and to Master Peascod, your father.**

BOTTOM: **Good Master Mustardseed, I know your patience well. That same cowardly, giantlike Oxbeef hath devoured many a gentleman of your house. I promise you, your kindred hath made my eyes water ere now. I desire your more acquaintance, good Master Mustardseed.**

Which fairy is not included? What might Bottom have said to that fairy?

AT 2:5

OBERON WAS PLEASED

Below is Puck's description of how he gave Bottom an ass's head, then led the other tradesmen around the forest, leaving Bottom on his own, to be found by Titania. Read the description first in Modern English, then in Shakespeare's English. Remember that Puck is really enjoying the mischief he has caused, and would be laughing as he speaks.

Modern English	Shakespeare's English
PUCK: *A group of clowns, rough working men, that work for their food in the market, were rehearsing their play which they hoped to put on for Duke Theseus on his wedding day. The most stupid one of all this stupid group, who was taking the part of Pyramus in their play, left their stage and went into a clump of trees. I followed him. I put an ass's head on his head. Soon, he went back to answer Thisbe. When the others saw him, they were frightened and ran away. I led them all over the forest, leaving Pyramus there, ass's head and all. And at that moment, Titania happened to wake up, and fell in love with the ass!*	PUCK: A crew of patches, rude mechanicals That work for bread upon Athenian stalls, Were met together to rehearse a play Intended for great Theseus' nuptial day. The shallowest thickskin of that barren sort, Who Pyramus presented, in their sport Forsook his scene and entered in a brake, When I did him at this advantage take An ass's nole I fixed on his head. Anon his Thisbe must be answered, And forth my mimic comes. When him they spy – So at his sight away his fellows fly... I led them on in this distracted fear, And left sweet Pyramus translated there; When in that moment – so it came to pass – Titania waked, and straightway loved an ass.

Point for Discussion

Oberon hoped that Titania would wake when some "vile[1] thing" was near. Was Bottom, even with the ass's head, a "vile thing"? Choose the words that describe Bottom. Can you think of any more?

amusing   repulsive   funny   grotesque   pathetic   attractive

[1] vile - very bad, horrible

AT 2:5

OBERON TRIED TO PUT THINGS RIGHT

Read the sentences below and put the correct names in the spaces.
You will need to use some names more than once.
Page 48 in *The Graphic Midsummer Night's Dream* will help you.
When you have finished, read your answers aloud.

1. Hermia told _____ to leave her alone.

2. Hermia thought _____ might have killed Lysander.

3. Oberon was angry with _____.

4. _____ had put the magic juice on _____ instead of Demetrius.

5. Puck was to go and find _____.

6. _____ was to be the first person Demetrius saw when he awoke.

7. _____ would love Helena.

8. Helena already loved _____. They would be happy.

Lysander   Hermia   Demetrius   Helena   Puck

AT 3:2

PUCK'S SENSE OF HUMOUR

Draw or cut and paste the pictures of Puck, Oberon, Helena and Demetrius in your notebook.
Write or cut and paste each speech beside the correct character. Practise saying the speeches with expression.
Puck is enjoying the mixed-up situation. He would be laughing at these foolish mortals[1].
Demetrius has fallen madly in love with Helena. Instead of being happy, Helena thinks they are making
fun of her. She is very angry.

OBERON

HELENA

DEMETRIUS

PUCK

OBERON: **Stand aside. The noise they make**
           Will cause Demetrius to awake.

PUCK: **Captain of our fairy band,**
           Helena is here at hand,
           And the youth mistook by me,
           Pleading for a lover's fee.
           Shall we their fond pageant see?
           Lord, what fools these mortals be!

PUCK: **Then will two at once woo one –**
           That must needs be sport alone;
           And those things do best please me
           That befall preposterously.

DEMETRIUS: *(Wakes)* **O Helen, goddess, nymph, perfect, divine –**
           To what, my love, shall I compare thine eyne?
           Crystal is muddy! O, how ripe in show
           Thy lips – those kissing cherries – tempting grow! O, let me kiss
           This princess of pure white, this seal of bliss!

HELENA: **O spite! O hell! I see you are all bent**
           To set against me for your merriment.
           If you were civil and knew courtesy
           You would not do me thus much injury.
           Can you not hate me – as I know you do –
           But you must join in souls to mock me too?
           If you were men – as men you are in show –
           You would not use a gentle lady so,
           To vow, and swear, and superpraise my parts,
           When, I am sure, you hate me with your hearts.

[1] mortals - human beings

AT 2:5

THINGS WENT WRONG AGAIN

The magic juice made both Lysander and Demetrius fall in love with Helena.
Before, they had both been in love with Hermia. That is why Helena could not believe they were serious.
Hermia could not believe that she had lost Lysander's love. Using the pictures below, draw arrows to show
who loved whom at the beginning of the play, and who loves who in Act 3, Scene 2.

HERMIA

DEMETRIUS

HELENA

LYSANDER

——————— **Beginning of the Play** ———————

HERMIA

DEMETRIUS

HELENA

LYSANDER

——————— **Act 3 Scene 2** ———————

THE QUARREL (1)

When people quarrel, they often call each other names.
Below are some of the things the lovers said to each other when they were quarrelling.
Look up the difficult words in a dictionary and add them to your word list. Read the lines aloud, then read
sentences 1 to 6 below. Put the number of each sentence beside the line(s) that it fits.

LYSANDER: *(to Hermia)* **Hang off, thou cat, thou burr! Vile thing, let loose,**
Or I will shake thee from me like a serpent.
.... – out, tawny Tartar, out;
Out loathed medicine! O hated potion, hence!

HERMIA: *(to Helena)* **O me, you juggler, you canker-blossom,**
You thief of love!

HELENA: *(to Hermia)* **Fie, fie, you counterfeit, you puppet, you**

HERMIA: *(to Helena)* **How low am I, thou painted maypole? Speak!**

HELENA: *(speaking about Hermia)*
She was a vixen when she went to school,
And though she be but little, she is fierce.

LYSANDER: *(to Hermia)* **Get you gone, you dwarf,**
You minimus of hindering knot-grass made,
You bead, you acorn.

Choose the lines that suggest:

1. Hermia had dark skin.

2. Hermia was not very tall.

3. Helena was quite tall.

4. Hermia could be violent.

5. Helena had stolen Lysander's love.

6. Hermia was holding on to Lysander.

Something to talk about:

When people quarrel, they sometimes say things they don't mean.
Have you ever said something in a quarrel that you have been sorry
about later? Write about it, or describe it to the class.

AT 2:5

THE QUARREL (2)

Copy or cut out and paste the two pictures below into your notebook. Read pages 52 and 54 in
The Graphic Midsummer Night's Dream.
On each page, there is a paragraph which describes what is happening in the picture.
Find the paragraph and write it under the picture.

AT 3:2

ANOTHER MISTAKE

Read the sentences below, and write them in your notebook. Decide which are True and which are False.
Page 56 in *The Graphic Midsummer Night's Dream* will help you.
When you have finished, read the sentences aloud.
Try making the False ones True, and the True ones False.

1. Lysander and Demetrius were fighting over Hermia.

2. Oberon and Puck saw them fighting.

3. Puck was very sorry about all the trouble he had caused.

4. Demetrius and Lysander were going to fight a duel.

5. Puck could imitate different voices.

6. Oberon gave Puck a different kind of magic juice.

7. Puck was to use it on Demetrius.

8. When Demetrius awoke, he would love Hermia as he did before.

9. Oberon planned to use the same juice on Titania.

10. Titania would soon forget her love for Oberon.

PUCK

OBERON

AT 3:2-4

— 28 —

TWO WEARY LADIES

This scene would be an excellent one to mime. Miming means acting without speaking. Try it first as a mime: think about the words but don't say them. Next, speak the words, but keep your good acting movements. You need five actors: Puck, Helena, Hermia, Demetrius and Lysander.

Lysander and Demetrius are already on the ground asleep. Puck stands by. Helena staggers in first. She looks both weary and very unhappy.

HELENA: **O weary night! O long and tedious night,**
　　　　　　Abate thy hours, shine comforts from the East,
　　　　　　She goes from one side of the stage to the other –
　　　　　　That I may back to Athens by daylight
　　　　　　From these that my poor company detest.
　　　　　　Sees Lysander and Demetrius. She starts to lie down far away from them, but Puck waves her closer to Demetrius. Helena moves almost like a puppet.
　　　　　　And sleep, that sometimes shuts up sorrow's eye,
　　　　　　Steal me a while from mine own company.

PUCK: *Mimes counting on his fingers –*
　　　　　　Yet but three? Come one more,
　　　　　　Two of both kinds make up four.
　　　　　　As Hermia comes in, Puck draws her along, waving her into position.
　　　　　　Here she comes, curst and sad.
　　　　　　Cupid is a knavish lad
　　　　　　Thus to make poor females mad.

HERMIA: *Hermia is crawling along, exhausted. Her hair, clothes, everything a mess.*
　　　　　　Never so weary, never so in woe,
　　　　　　Bedabbled with the dew, and torn with briars –
　　　　　　She sits and looks at her legs and arms, all covered with scratches.
　　　　　　I can no further crawl, no further go.
　　　　　　My legs can keep no pace with my desires.
　　　　　　She too starts to lie down, but is directed to a different spot, closer to Lysander, by Puck. She slowly stretches out. Her last words are spoken as if she is talking in her sleep –
　　　　　　Here will I rest me till the break of day.
　　　　　　Heavens shield Lysander if they mean a fray.

PUCK: *Puck dances around as if he were weaving a spell with these words, going from Demetrius to Helena, and Hermia to Lysander, ending at Lysander –*
　　　　　　On the ground
　　　　　　Sleep sound.
　　　　　　I'll apply
　　　　　　To your eye,
　　　　　　Gentle lover, remedy.
　　　　　　Puck stoops over Lysander and squeezes juice onto Lysander's eyelids –
　　　　　　When thou wakest,
　　　　　　Thou takes
　　　　　　True delight
　　　　　　In the sight
　　　　　　Of thy former lady's eye.

　　　　　　He skips from Lysander to Hermia and back again, weaving the spell –
　　　　　　And the country proverb known,
　　　　　　That every man should take his own,
　　　　　　In your waking shall be shown.
　　　　　　He points from Hermia to Lysander, Demetrius to Helena, and exits, calling the last line as he is almost offstage –
　　　　　　Jack shall have Jill;
　　　　　　Naught shall go ill.
　　　　　　The man shall have his mare again, and all shall be well.

AT 2:5

TITANIA AWOKE FROM HER DREAM

Read the questions below, and answer them in good sentences.
When you have finished, read your answers aloud.
Pages 44 and 60 in *The Graphic Midsummer Night's Dream* will help you.

1. Who looked after Bottom and made sure he had a wonderful time?

2. What were the names of the fairies? (Look at page 44 if you are not sure.)

3. Why was Oberon happy?

4. Why did Oberon put some juice on Titania's eyelids?

5. When Titania awoke, how did she feel about Bottom?

6. Who took away the ass's head from Bottom?

7. Why did the fairies have to hurry away?

8. Who told Titania what had happened?

Cut out the pictures below, and paste them in your notebook.
Under each character, print or paste the words they said.

PUCK	BOTTOM	TITANIA	OBERON

There lies your love.	I shall desire you of more acquaintance, good Master Cobweb.
How come these things to pass? O, how mine eyes do loathe his visage now.	I'll apply To your eye, Gentle lover, remedy.

AT 3:3

DUKE THESEUS WENT HUNTING

> Fill in the spaces in the sentences below with the correct names.
> When you have finished, read your sentences aloud.
> If you need help, read page 62 in *The Graphic Midsummer Night's Dream*.

1. _____ and _____ were hunting in the forest.

2. Hermia's father, _____, was hunting with them.

3. _____, _____, _____, and _____ were sleeping on the ground.

4. To wake them, the _____ sounded their horns.

5. Egeus was angry because _____ had tried to run away.

6. Now there were three happy couples:

   _____ and _____
   _____ and _____
   _____ and _____

7. _____ decided that there would be no hunting that day.

8. The three _____ would all be married together.

9. They went to prepare for the _____.

10. Later that day, _____ returned to his friends.

> Cut out the pictures below. Paste them in your notebook with the happy couples in pairs.

DEMETRIUS

HERMIA

LYSANDER

HELENA

THESEUS

HIPPOLYTA

AT 3:2

QUINCE'S PROLOGUE

The main reason for speaking and writing in sentences, is to make our meaning clear.
In writing, the sentences are separated by full stops and capital letters.
Look at the paragraph below, which is taken from page 64 in *The Graphic Midsummer Night's Dream*.
The full stops and capital letters have been changed. Read it aloud.
Does it make sense? Correct it by putting the full stops and capital letters in the right places.
Now read it aloud. Does it make better sense?

Peter Quince read his prologue he was so nervous. That he stopped. In all the wrong places his prologue didn't really. Make sense the nobles thought. It was funny they interrupted. And made loud comments.

Below are some sentences without any punctuation.
Write them with full stops and capital letters in the correct places. Read your sentences aloud.

1. it was the night of the wedding Theseus decided they would watch the tradesmen's play

2. Titania awoke she hated Bottom now

3. there was a mischievous fairy called Puck he played tricks on people

4. the king of the fairies was called Oberon Titania was the queen of the fairies

5. the fairies looked after Bottom he had a wonderful time

6. the huntsmen sounded their horns the lovers woke up

AT 3:2

Putting on *The Comedy of Pyramus and Thisbe* For a Year or School Assembly

This scene makes an excellent one act play, just as it is written. Begin from Quince's Prologue (line 108) down to Theseus' speech (line 360),

THESEUS: **A fortnight hold we this solemnity**
In nightly revels and new jollity.

You will need eleven actors altogether – the six ladies and gentlemen (Hippolyta, Theseus, Lysander, Hermia, Demetrius, Helena) who sit close to or even on the 'stage' – and the five tradesmen.

Here are some suggestions to help you.

Things to Remember When Putting on a Play

1. **The Script** Ask your teacher to photocopy the play of *Pyramus and Thisbe*, Act 5 scene 1, with a copy for each actor. This is your script. Each actor underlines or highlights their lines. Any play is better if the actors learn their lines really well. If you really find it impossible to memorise, you may look at a script, but you shouldn't have to read every word. The audience will get very bored if they have to listen to you read.

2. **Costumes** Shakespeare's actors wore the clothes of their own time, so you can too. If you wish to wear costumes, the drawings in *The Graphic Midsummer Night's Dream* will help you, or design your own.

3. **Rehearsals** Have as many rehearsals as possible. Divide the play into short sections, so that small groups of actors can work together. Make sure that everyone knows about the rehearsals well in advance, including when and where they are to be held.

REHEARSAL
PYRAMUS AND THISBE

TRADESMEN ONLY
(QUINCE, BOTTOM, FLUTE, SNOUT, STARVELING)

12:30 p.m. Tuesday, January 16
Ms Evans' Room – 106

Be on time!

AT 2:5

Putting on a Play: Who does What?

- **Director**

  The Director plans how the play will be staged. (S)he takes charge of rehearsals, suggesting to the actors where and how they might move, and how they say their lines. A good director will plan all this in advance. After the first couple of rehearsals, the Director interrupts the actors as little as possible. (S)he makes notes as the actors rehearse and discusses them with the actors at the end of each run-through. The Director should be ready to listen to the actors if they have ideas about how the play should go.

- **Assistant Director**

  The Assistant Director helps the Director as much as possible. (S)he schedules rehearsals, makes sure that all the actors are informed, and circulates notices. If necessary, the Assistant Director can take extra rehearsals to work on some particular aspect, such as clear speech, or memorising lines.

- **Stage Manager**

  The Stage Manager makes sure that the stage is properly arranged: that furniture (chairs, cushions etc) are in the right place. Wine glasses, and trays of fruit, could be used to suggest a banquet. These things would be the job of the Stage Manager.

- **Publicity Manager**

  The Publicity Manager plans the publicity materials for the play, such as notices or posters and makes sure they are put up around the school. The Publicity Manager is also responsible for programmes, if you are having them. Be sure that your programmes include a "thank you" to people who have given you extra help, for example:

  Form 9C would like to thank:
  Mrs Pauline Webster, our Site Manager
  Ms Ann Evans, our Form Tutor
  Mr Rodney Brown, our Art Teacher
  for all their help in staging this production.

DON'T MISS IT!

Form 9C's Production of

The Comedy of Pyramus and Thisbe

by

William Shakespeare

Year 9 Assembly   **Friday, 24 February, 2000**

Shakespeare's Adjectives

The name of a person, place, or thing is a ***noun*** – for example: book, tree, house, girl, boy.

An ***adjective*** is a word that tells us more about a noun –
a *thick* book, a *leafy* tree, a *white* house, a *lively* girl, a *popular* boy.
thick   leafy   white   lively   popular are all adjectives.

Choosing your adjectives very carefully helps to make your writing more interesting.
Look at some of Shakespeare's adjectives below:

THESEUS   *(to Hermia, Act 1 Scene 1, line 71)*
For aye to be in *shady* cloister mewed,
To live a *barren* sister all your life,
Chanting *faint* hymns to the *cold*, *fruitless* moon.

LYSANDER   *(speaking about Helena and Demetrius, Act 1, Scene 1, line 107)*
and she, *sweet* lady, dotes,
Devoutly dotes, dotes in idolatry
Upon this *spotted* and *inconstant* man.

How would you describe Shakespeare's adjectives? Choose the best words from:
ordinary   unusual   boring   well-chosen   interesting

THESEUS   LYSANDER

In the sentences below, choose the adjective *that you prefer* from the words in brackets. Note, you may choose more than one if you wish:

1. Old Mrs Jones was a (delightful   beloved   nice) member of the community.
2. The house on the hill had an (frightening   bad   intimidating) reputation.
3. The P.E. teacher had a (loud   shrill   thunderous) voice.
4. The tropical sunset glowed with (glorious   vibrant   pretty) colours.
5. In the school canteen, we get (delicious   disgusting   nourishing) food.

> Look at the Key Speeches on pages 11, 13, 23, 31, 35, and 43 in *The Graphic Midsummer Night's Dream*.
> Can you find more examples of Shakespeare's adjectives?

AT 3:3

Shakespeare's Adverbs

A **verb** is a word that usually describes an action, such as:

        John **ran**.   Titania **awoke**.

An **adverb** gives us more information about the verb, for example:

        John ran **quickly**.   Titania awoke **suddenly**.

Many adverbs end in **ly**, but quite a lot do not, for example:

        John ran **fast**.

Choosing your adverbs very carefully helps to make your writing more interesting.
Look at some of Shakespeare's adverbs:

BOTTOM: *(Act 1, Scene 2 line 99)*
        We will meet, and there we may rehearse most *obscenely*[1] and *courageously*.

HERMIA: *(to Lysander, Act 2, Scene 2, line 59)*
        Lysander riddles very *prettily*.

HELENA: *(looking for Lysander, Act 2, Scene 2, line 162)*
        Either death or you I'll find *immediately*.

PUCK: *(joking about the muddle he has caused, Act 3, Scene 2, line 120)*
        And those things do best please me
        That befall *preposterously*.

OBERON: *(to Puck, Act 3, Scene 2, line 345)*
        Still thou mistakest,
        Or else committest thy knaveries *wilfully*.

From the list given, choose the best adverb given for each of the spaces below.
When you have finished, read your sentences aloud.

| *thirstily* | *greedily* | *painfully* | *fast* | *wearily* |
| *faster* | *slowly* | *happily* | *quickly* | *briskly* |

He ran home _____.

The soldiers marched _____.

_____we returned home.

Kiron ran _____ down the hill.

George ran _____, but Mary ran _____.

Hermia drank the water _____.

Imran was very hungry and ate _____.

Old Mr Williams walked _____ and _____.

[1] obscenely - means in a very rude way. This is not what Bottom intended to say

AT 3:3

A Map of the Forest

Plan an imaginery map showing where some of the events in *A Midsummer Night's Dream* took place.
Draw or cut out and paste a small picture at each place that you put on your map.

ATHENS  Theseus's Palace.

THE FOREST

Titania fell asleep.

Lysander and Hermia fell asleep.

Tradesmen rehearsed "Pyramus and Thisbe".

Lysander, Demetrius, Helena and Hermia fell asleep.

Titania and her fairies gave Bottom a wonderful time.

Theseus and Hermia went hunting.

A Midsummer Night's Dream Word Search

How many of these words can you find?

THESEUS, FAIRIES, TITANIA, CARPENTER, SNOUT, FOREST, ATHENS, TINKER, OBERON, QUINCE, THISBE, PUCK, HUNTING, DEMETRIUS, TRADESMEN, PYRAMUS, FLUTE, NUNNERY, MOTH, HELENA, MOONSHINE, LYSANDER, BOTTOM, PEASEBLOSSOM, MAGIC, HIPPOLYTA, SNUG, PROLOGUE, HERMIA, PLAY, WALL, SHAKESPEARE, EGEUS, STARVELING, MUSTARDSEED

C	A	R	P	E	N	T	E	R	Y	Q	M	S	P	H	E
A	T	H	E	S	E	U	S	D	B	J	H	X	U	E	L
U	H	I	F	K	E	T	N	Y	M	A	G	I	C	R	O
R	E	G	N	M	L	B	O	T	T	O	M	Z	K	M	K
N	N	S	Y	K	F	L	U	T	E	I	O	A	T	I	N
M	S	F	A	P	E	M	T	H	I	L	P	N	Z	A	U
P	Y	N	H	M	V	R	E	R	T	A	O	S	N	O	N
E	G	E	U	S	Q	Y	K	P	N	R	A	F	R	M	N
O	T	S	N	G	S	H	A	K	E	S	P	E	A	R	E
M	D	R	T	M	T	M	Y	B	P	K	D	A	V	X	R
E	E	F	I	U	A	W	O	S	G	Y	S	P	L	A	Y
E	M	V	N	F	R	P	R	O	L	O	G	U	E	M	H
H	E	B	G	Q	V	A	Y	A	N	G	J	E	M	T	Z
M	T	M	L	E	E	U	T	X	L	S	K	V	O	S	D
U	R	W	A	L	L	H	E	I	V	U	H	M	A	M	A
S	I	M	Z	M	I	C	T	F	A	I	R	I	E	S	T
T	U	O	F	S	N	Q	B	E	U	M	N	P	N	S	P
A	S	T	B	I	G	A	Q	P	I	A	R	N	E	E	Y
R	J	E	U	K	N	M	L	L	T	R	V	R	J	M	R
D	N	Q	A	E	Q	W	H	I	P	P	O	L	Y	T	A
S	Z	K	L	P	Y	P	T	M	O	F	W	D	E	M	M
E	V	E	H	Y	M	L	Y	S	A	N	D	E	R	O	U
E	H	N	T	R	A	D	E	S	M	E	N	M	S	K	S
D	S	P	E	A	S	E	B	L	O	S	S	O	M	C	M

Points of View
The Night in the Forest

Write about the night in the forest from the point of view of one of the main characters: Helena, Hermia, Lysander, Demetrius, Bottom, Titania, Oberon or Puck. Three of the characters, Lysander, Demetrius, and Titania had the "love juice" put on their eyes. Two of those, Lysander and Titania, also had the "forgetting" juice used on their eyes. How do you think this would affect their memory? Would they remember as clearly as the others, or would their remembrances be muddled? Remember that Titania had Oberon's explanation to help her, but Lysander had no such help.
Write in the first person, that is, from the point of view of "I". Some suggestions are given below to help you.
Read your stories aloud to the class. Remember, you are the character speaking your thoughts.
You could dress in costume, if you wish. Read your stories at a year or school assembly.

BOTTOM: That night in the forest was the most wonderful night of my life. I really don't know how it happened, but I will try to tell you what I remember. First of all, I got a very hairy face. It felt most strange. And every time I tried to speak, I went, "Hee-haw!" just like a donkey. Quince and the rest ran away from me, shouting into the forest. As I was walking up and down, singing a song to cheer myself up, this beautiful woman appeared and said that she loved me. Well, then things really got interesting

TITANIA: Oberon and I were having an awful row. It started because he wanted my little Indian boy to be his servant. The boy's mother had been my friend. Now she was dead, but for her sake, I wanted to look after her child. Oberon couldn't understand why I wouldn't give up the boy. He was furious. We met in the forest, and said a lot of nasty things to each other. That night, I had the strangest dream. I met a funny creature with a hairy face....

LYSANDER: There are some things about that strange night in the forest that I guess I'll never figure out. Hermia and I were there in the first place because we had decided to run away together. Hermia's father, Egeus, wanted her to marry Demetrius. Egeus even went to Duke Theseus. The law of Athens was that Hermia had to do as her father said. If she didn't she could be put to death, or be sent away forever to a nunnery. We decided to run away. We met in the forest, as we had decided to do....

PUCK: I've never had so much fun in my life. That night in the forest was amazing. I put the magic love juice on the eyes of the wrong man, and the mortals got so muddled, I laughed and laughed. I had the most fun of all with the tradesmen. I happened to see them rehearsing....

BOTTOM

TITANIA   LYSANDER

PUCK

AT 3:4-5

DESKTOP TEACHING

This is a whole-class exercise to make sure that everyone understands some of the things you have learned about the play. First, students who are sure they can answer a particular question take the Desktop Teaching card. They put the cards on their desks where they can be clearly seen. Everyone tries to answer the questions themselves, using the Answer Sheet on page 41. If you are not sure about an answer, visit the "Desktop Teacher" who will explain it to you. You should then be able to write good, complete answers to the questions.

WHY WERE OBERON AND TITANIA HAVING A ROW?

WHY WAS EGEUS ANGRY WITH HERMIA?

WHY DID OBERON PLAN TO USE THE LOVE JUICE ON DEMETRIUS?

"HE'S A GOOD ACTOR, BUT HE DRIVES ME CRAZY. HE'S ALWAYS SHOWING OFF!" WHO WOULD PETER QUINCE BE TALKING ABOUT? WHY?

DUKE THESEUS DECIDED TO MARRY QUEEN HIPPOLYTA. THE PEOPLE OF ATHENS MIGHT HAVE BEEN SURPRISED. WHY?

ACCORDING TO THE LAW OF ATHENS, WHAT WERE THE PUNISHMENTS FOR A DAUGHTER WHO DISOBEYED HER FATHER?

WHAT, IN YOUR OPINION, WAS PUCK'S BIGGEST MISTAKE? WAS HE TRULY SORRY FOR THE TROUBLE HE CAUSED?

IN YOUR OPINION, WHY DID HELENA NOT BELIEVE THAT DEMETRIUS AND LYSANDER BOTH LOVED HER?

EXPLAIN HOW TITANIA, QUEEN OF THE FAIRIES, CAME TO FALL IN LOVE WITH AN ASS.

OBERON AND PUCK USED A "FORGETTING" JUICE ON TWO PEOPLE, TO TAKE AWAY THE EFFECT OF THE FIRST JUICE. WHO WERE THESE PEOPLE? WHAT WAS THE RESULT IN EACH CASE?

AT THE END OF THE PLAY, THERE WERE FOUR HAPPY COUPLES. WHO WERE THEY?

WHAT IS "ALLITERATION"? CAN YOU GIVE THREE EXAMPLES FROM THE PLAY?

DESKTOP TEACHING - Answer Sheet

NAME_____   FORM:_____

Remember to write your answers in good sentences.

1. Why were Oberon and Titania having a row?

    _____
    _____.

2. Why was Egeus angry with Hermia?

    _____
    _____.

3. Why did Oberon decide to use the love juice on Demetrius?

    _____
    _____.

4. "He's a good actor, but he drives me crazy. He's always showing off!" Who might Peter Quince be talking about? Why?

    _____
    _____.

5. Duke Theseus decided to marry Queen Hippolyta. The people of Athens might have been surprised. Why?

    _____
    _____.

6. According to the law of Athens, what were the punishments for a daughter who disobeyed her father?

    _____
    _____.

7. What, in your opinion, was Puck's biggest mistake? Was he truly sorry for the trouble he caused?

    _____
    _____.

8. In your opinion, why did Helena not believe that Demetrius and Lysander both loved her?

    _____
    _____.

9. Explain how Titania, Queen of the Fairies, came to fall in love with an ass.

    _____
    _____.

10. Oberon and Puck used a "forgetting" juice on two people, to take away the effect of the first juice. Who were these two people? What was the result in each case?

    _____
    _____.

11. At the end of the play, there were four happy couples. Who were they?

    _____
    _____.

12. What is "alliteration"? Can you give three examples from the play?

    _____
    _____.

THE 'WHO AM I?' GAME

You need 5 activity sheets for this game, including this one. Prepare for the 'Who Am I' game as follows:

1. Paste each set of characters onto a separate card.

2. Add the appropriate portrait from the picture gallery.

3. Number the cards, the order is not important, and write the names and numbers on a master sheet: (for example: 1. Oberon 2. Lysander 3. Puck)

4. Make up individual score cards as shown below.

NAME:		
CARD No.	POINTS SCORED	TOTAL
	GRAND TOTAL	

Rules of the Game

1. Working in pairs, one student holds the card with the blank side facing the partner. The partner asks questions that can be answered 'Yes' or 'No'.

   For example: *'Are you a tradesman?'*
                 'Do you enjoy causing mischief?'

2. Each question counts as one point.

3. Each direct question about the name of a character counts 5 points if the answer is 'No'.
   For example: *'Are you Oberon?'* counts 5 points if the answer is no. This is to stop you simply guessing, hoping to get lucky!

4. Clues may be offered, one at a time, in return for a small 'price' of two points.
   At the request, *'Please give me a clue'*, one of the clues on the card is read out, and two points are added to the score.

5. Mark the points on your score card as you go along. Add up the points on each line for the 'Total' column as you identify each character.

Take turns holding the cards and asking the questions. Remember, the aim is to guess the name of the character while getting the **lowest** number of points.

CHARACTER CLUES

Lysander

Paste portrait here

> Hermia's father didn't like me.
> Hermia and I decided to run away together.
> I had a rich aunt. She thought of me as her son.
> I have vague memories of being in love with Helena.
> Demetrius and I were going to fight a duel.
> In the end, I married Hermia.

Oberon

Paste portrait here

> I wanted a little Indian boy to be my servant.
> I remembered a magic juice that could make people fall in love with the first person they saw.
> I was furious with Titania when she wouldn't give me the Indian boy.
> I made Titania fall in love with an ass!
> I tried to help Helena, but Puck made a mess of it all.

Helena

Paste portrait here

> I loved Demetrius. I loved him more than anything.
> Hermia and I had been friends since we were little girls.
> I told Demetrius that Hermia and Lysander were planning to run away.
> The more Demetrius hated me, the more I loved him.
> I was sure that Demetrius and Lysander were only pretending to be in love with me. They were joking.
> I was sure that Hermia was in on the joke as well.

Flute

Paste portrait here

> I have a beard coming.
> I didn't think I should have to play the part of a woman.
> I played the part of Thisbe.
> Pyramus and I had to whisper through a hole in a wall.
> At the end of *Pyramus and Thisbe*, I killed myself.

Puck

Paste portrait here

> I serve Oberon, King of the Fairies.
> I can imitate human voices.
> I put the love juice on the eyes of the wrong man.
> Helena, Demetrius, Lysander and Hermia, got into a terrible muddle. I thought it was very funny.
> I put an ass's head on Bottom. That was very funny, too.
> I led Demetrius and Lysander all through the forest, to stop them fighting a duel.

CHARACTER CLUES

Duke Theseus

Paste portrait
here

> I ruled Athens.
> I fought against the Amazons.
> I fell in love with Hippolyta, Queen of the Amazons.
> I planned a wonderful wedding.
> I told Hermia that she had to obey her father.
> I enjoy hunting.

Hermia

Paste portrait
here

> My father was very angry with me.
> I loved Lysander.
> I ran away with Lysander.
> Suddenly, Lysander didn't love me any more!
> I woke up in the woods, all alone.
> I hated Helena for taking Lysander away from me.
> In the end, I married Lysander.

Demetrius

Paste portrait
here

> A long time ago, I thought I loved Helena.
> For a while, I loved Hermia.
> Hermia's father wanted her to marry me.
> I followed Hermia and Lysander into the woods.
> For a while, I thought Helena was a pest.
> In the end, I married Helena.

Titania
Paste portrait
here

> I was the Queen of the Fairies.
> I had a terrible row with Oberon.
> Oberon wanted my friend's little boy to be his servant.
> Oberon told me that I had been in love with an ass!
> Oberon and I blessed the three couples after their wedding.

Hippolyta

Paste portrait
here

> I fought against Duke Theseus in battle.
> I enjoy hunting.
> I was Queen of the Amazons.
> I fell in love with Duke Theseus.
> I married Duke Theseus.
> My people were defeated by Duke Theseus.

CHARACTER CLUES

Starveling Paste portrait here	> I am a tailor. I make clothes. > I played Moonshine in *Pyramus and Thisbe*. > My name sounds as if I don't get much to eat. > I had to have a lantern, a bush and a dog.
Snout Paste portrait here	> I am a tinker. I mend pots and pans. > In *Pyramus and Thisbe* I played the part of Wall. > I had to hold my fingers to make the hole in the wall. > Pyramus and Thisbe had to whisper through my fingers.
Snug Paste portrait here	> I am a joiner. I make furniture, cupboards, and things. > I was Lion in *Pyramus and Thisbe* > I didn't have any lines to learn in the play. > All I had to do was roar! > I told all the people that I wasn't really a lion.
Bottom Paste portrait here	> I am the best actor in our group. > I could probably have played all the parts in our play. > For a while, I kept making noises like a donkey. > The beautiful Fairy Queen was in love with me. > All the pretty fairies were bringing me fruit, and stroking my hairy face! > I played Pyramus in *The Comedy of Pyramus and Thisbe*. > At the end of the play, I told all the people that I wasn't really dead.
Egeus Paste portrait here	> I had an argument with my daughter. > I asked Duke Theseus to settle the argument. > I was angry when I found my daughter sleeping in the forest. > I wanted my daughter to marry Demetrius. > I didn't want my daughter to marry Lysander.
Quince Paste portrait here	> I chose the people to play the different parts in *Pyramus and Thisbe*. > Bottom was always interfering and bossing everyone around. > I read my Prologue at the beginning of the play. > When I read my Prologue, I was very nervous. > When I read my Prologue, I stopped in all the wrong places. > I was very worried when Bottom disappeared.

PORTRAIT GALLERY

Cut around dotted lines and paste portraits on to the character clue cards

Oberon

Hippolyta

Theseus

Titania

Lysander

Hermia

Demetrius

Helena

Egeus

Puck

Bottom

Quince

Flute

Starveling

Snout

Snug

A MIDSUMMER NIGHT'S DREAM

RECORD OF MY WORK

Name: _____   Form: _____

Date started: _____   Date completed: _____

TITLE AND NUMBER OF ACTIVITY	How well did you do this activity?			Was it easy or difficult?			TEACHER'S OR PUPIL'S COMMENTS
	Very Well	Quite Well	I could have tried harder	Too difficult	Too easy	Just right	

WHAT THINGS HAVE I IMPROVED?

Writing in sentences, using full stops and capital letters	
Writing in a more interesting way	
Spelling	
Understanding Shakespeare's English	
Acting and speaking Shakespeare's English	
What did I enjoy about *A Midsummer Night's Dream?*	
What went well with my work?	
Other things I should be trying to improve	